Teacher

Lucy M. George   Ando Twin

Miss Betts cycles to school early in the morning. She waves hello to Andy. He helps people to cross the road.

Before the children arrive, Miss Betts gets everything ready for the day.

Mr Fletcher, the classroom assistant, asks what he can do to help.

It's time for school to start. The bell rings and the children come in and sit down.

"Good morning, Miss Betts!" they say together.

Miss Betts has some exciting news. A very special guest is coming to visit the class later today.

Mr Fletcher takes the children to their assembly.

Today it is about trying your best and not giving up.

In the morning, Miss Betts teaches maths.

$$7 \quad\quad 6$$
$$+\ 3 \quad +\ 4$$
$$\quad\quad\quad = 10$$

After playtime, the class goes to the library.

Then they go back to class
to do some painting.

Finally, it's lunchtime!

Miss Betts encourages Sophie to try some peas
and helps Toby find his lunch box.

"I'd better go and meet our special guest now!"
says Miss Betts with a smile.

The special guest is Kelly Jones,
a local athlete and 100 metre gold medalist!

The children are very excited! They hurry into
their PE kits and go out to the field.

Kelly shows them how to do star jumps...

...and push ups to warm up.

Then they have a race.

"Try your best and don't give up!" Kelly shouts.

Afterwards they sit on the grass and ask Kelly questions.

She tells them what it's like to be an athlete...

...how she won her gold medal...

...and what kinds of food she eats to stay healthy.

"Do you want to try on my medal?" she asks.

There's time for one more race – between the grown-ups!

Mr Crawford, the head teacher, comes out to watch.

Kelly Jones wins the race!

"Hooray!" everyone cheers.

Back in the classroom, Miss Betts
reads the children a story...

...and then it's home time.

The children wave
goodbye to Miss Betts
and Mr Fletcher.

"See you tomorrow, everyone!"
Miss Betts says.

Mr Fletcher helps Miss Betts tidy up and they talk about their plans for tomorrow. It's going to be another busy day!

On her way home, Miss Betts has to ride up a big hill. Some days she has to stop because it's very steep.

But she remembers Kelly Jones saying,

"Try your best and don't give up!"

And guess what?

Today, she makes it all the way to the top!

What else does Miss Betts do?

Writes
reports.

Holds
parents'
evenings.

Plans
lessons.

Marks
homework.

Puts the children's
work on display.

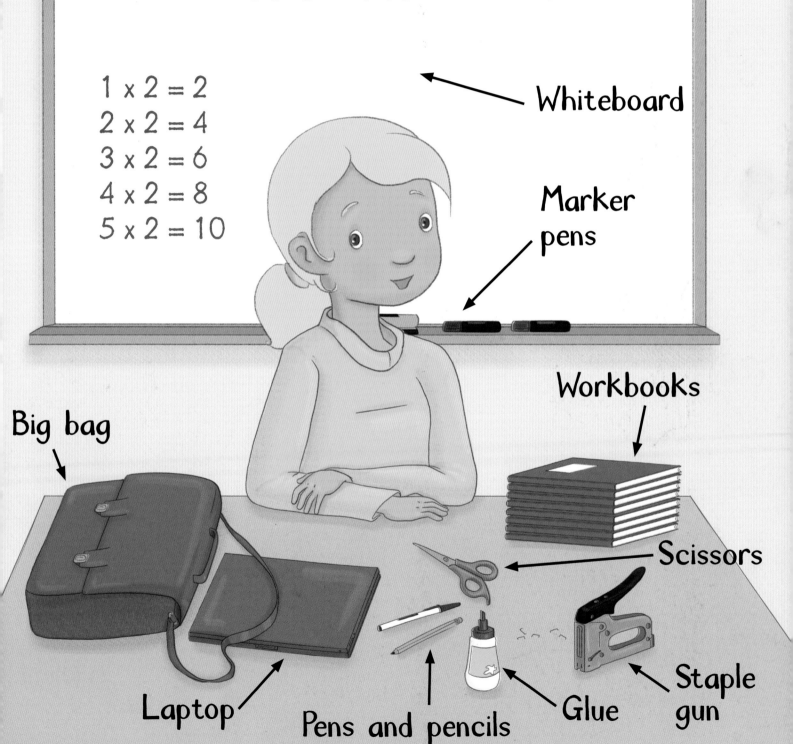

Other busy people

Here are some of the other busy people teachers work with.

Classroom assistants help the children with their work during lessons. They also help the teacher to prepare materials and tidy up.

Head teachers are in charge of running the school. They meet with parents and other teachers to make sure all the children are happy and learning.

Lunchtime monitors help the school chefs serve hot and cold meals for the children and staff. They also help to look after the children in the lunch hall and in the playground.

Crossing guards help children to cross the road safely on their way to school and on their way back home.

Next steps

- Can the children remember what Miss Betts and her class did during their busy day? Talk to the children about their experiences at school. What are their favourite lessons and why?

- Talk to the children about the other busy people in the book. Which of these jobs would the children like to do and why?

- Talk to the children about the visit from Kelly Jones. Have the children ever met a professional sportsperson? What sports do they like? Do they have any sporting heroes?

- Kelly Jones won her medals because she tried her hardest and didn't give up. Discuss this with the children. Have they ever tried really hard at something?

- On her way home, Miss Betts managed to ride all the way up a steep hill. Did the children think she'd make it? If so, why?

Quarto is the authority on a wide range of topics.

Quarto educates, entertains and enriches the lives of our readers—enthusiasts and lovers of hands-on living.

www.quartoknows.com

Publisher: Zeta Jones
Associate Publisher: Maxime Boucknooghe
Editorial Director: Victoria Garrard
Art Director: Laura Roberts-Jensen
Editor: Sophie Hallam
Designer: Anna Lubecka

Copyright © QED Publishing 2015

First published in the UK in 2015 by
QED Publishing
Part of The Quarto Group,
The Old Brewery,
6 Blundell Street,
London, N7 9BH

www.quartoknows.com/brand/2040/QED-Publishing/

A catalogue record for this book is available from the British Library.

ISBN 978 1 78493 154 4

Printed in China

**For Granny Wilson
- AndoTwin**

**For Milo Theodore Betts
- Lucy M.George**